There's A Squirrel In My Kitchen!!

By

Laurie Janz

Dedication

As this book was written, I had countless friends in mind to dedicate this book to. I have been blessed with so many friends over the years. Too many to mention, but I will mention some of them at the top of my list, who helped and prayed for my family and me, and were always there when I needed a lift. They are in no special order, but were either family, friends, or inspirational in my life.

Audrey H., Linda K., Jane W., Nancy M., Elizabeth H., Hazel S., Donna W., Carol E., Jackie G., and a special thanks to my lovely niece, Leah S.! There are so many more names, too many to mention, but just the same, always there for me! May God bless you all and your families. I love you!!!

About the Author

I am a devoted Christian, living my dream life with my wonderful husband. God gave us two of the best sons we could have asked for. Joshua and Caleb, we have four beautiful grandchildren and one on the way. As for me, I am trying to beat a brain tumor, which gets the best of me some days. But my husband, children, family, friends, and a few doctors are doing their best to help me beat this terrible disease. I ask God, numerous times, why me? I've given a great part of my life to the church and teaching Bible study with the children. I've been a BSF member, worked at the Christian Coalition, Goodwill, and the Christian Service Center in St Augustine. I pray daily for many, and also pray that if God is going to take me from my family. He watches over them 'til we meet again.

It was a warm summer evening. My husband and I were out in front of our house, just relaxing and feeding our two dogs before we took our evening walk. Suddenly, our cat appeared to be sneaking down the driveway, kind of like a sniper. But in the next minute or two, our cat came running up the driveway with something in her mouth. She made a beeline to the backyard, and I just had to see what she had hanging from her mouth.

So I told my husband I would be right back after I saw what the cat had run off with. I scolded the cat, and she dropped whatever she had in her mouth and ran away. When I bent over to see what it was, I picked up a tiny little creature that turned out to be a baby squirrel. She didn't even have her eyes open yet.

So I went back to show my husband what the cat had in her mouth. We never knew what was in store for us, but this little creature was about to take control of my life for years to come. We put the dogs up and headed to the pet store to find some type of milk and food she could survive on. We did get some type of formula and some syringes and headed back home.

So once we got back home, I set up a little home for her, made from a shoebox. I stuffed it with cotton balls and soft tissues and made it as cozy as I could. For the next several weeks, I fed her every four hours, night and day. I didn't sleep some nights, come to think of it, neither did my husband, might be because of the alarm going off?

My husband always comes up with names for our pets. I think he realized that this little squirrel was going to be with us for a while. So he named her "Skippy". Skippy soon started to open her eyes, and I have no idea what she expected to see as she opened her eyes, but I'm pretty sure she wasn't expecting my face.

But it was love at first sight. I became her mother and best friend that day. She was about to change my life for quite some time. Over the next few weeks, she watched me like a hawk. She would nap for a while, but when she woke up, she panicked until she saw me. I would pick her up and hold her to comfort her.

Skippy had several homes over the next few weeks as she grew and got braver and curious and checked out the world a little. I didn't want her to go outside. I was afraid our cat or some other varmint would grab her. So she graduated from the shoebox to a pirate's hat and several other homes we made for her.

Well, as time went on, she found a way to our screened porch. We bought her another house to live in. It was a wooden box where she would come and go from. We actually bought several of these over the next few months and had a few inside our house, where she could hide things and sleep a little too.

Well, the screen porch was great for a little while. Until she saw other squirrels running up and down the trees and in the yard. Skippy wanted so bad to go out and play with the other squirrels, but I was afraid to let her out. I thought if I did, she would never come back inside. So for the time being, she would sit by the screen and watch patiently as her soon-to-be friends ran up and down and all around.

Skippy had some sharp teeth, and she never used them on me, but she started to use them on the screens. She would chew holes in the screen, and my husband and I tried to stop her and patch some of the holes she started, but soon we gave up, maybe because Skippy would chew on my husband's fingers if he tried to stop her.

I even tried to bring the outside in our screened porch, by cutting branches and tree limbs and putting them in and around her newest house, which was a four-foot cage we could keep her in and close so she couldn't chew on the screens. But like everything else, she wanted more. She loved the branches. We tried to get branches that had acorns on them, and she did like that.

Then the day came when we decided to let her go outside. They say "D" day was the longest day. But I think the day Skippy was let out was my longest day. Skippy was happier than a kid on Christmas Day. She was a natural climber. She ran up and down the trees and jumped from tree to tree with ease. I think I aged a few years, and gray hairs started to spring up here and there in my long hair.

Skippy rolled in the dirt, jumped and played in the birdbath, and had a ball all day. Other squirrels would watch her from a distance. I think they knew she came from inside our house and probably thought she was something special, but it didn't take long for a few other squirrels to come check her out. They came face to face and barked at each other a little, and soon would fight a bit.

Of course, I worried about her safety and tried to get her to come back inside. She would have no part of it. She continued to run and play, while I tried to get her to come back inside. I would go out into the yard and call her to come to me. She did come close enough to jump on me, which she has done many times in the house, but not outside.

So when my husband came home from work, we put some of her favorite vegetables on a tray to persuade her to come in. She must have been hungry and tired, and soon I got her in my hands, and we opened the door and got her back in her cage and shut the door. But I think she had a good first day outside and was fine after we brought her back inside.

Skippy and I were close and had quite a bond together. She was quite a curious creature. She loved running up and down my arms. She would just lie in my lap, while I rubbed her belly and played with her, kind of like mothers do, right? We would play for a while, and eventually she

would get tired, and I'd let her curl up and keep her warm
and comfy 'til she fell asleep.

One of my sons had a bulldog named Meaty. Meaty loved to chew on those rawhide bones, and guess what? Skippy did too. Meaty was a good sport and would share his rawhide with Skippy. Meaty would just look at her and probably wondered why she liked them, while Skippy wondered if Meaty would eat her!!

Meaty and Skippy actually got along quite well. Skippy had this thing about jumping on us, and she also would jump on Meaty and catch a ride around the house. As long as Skippy was busy inside, she didn't seem to think about going outside. She played and ran up and down our steps and in and out of our house. You never knew when she'd show up.

While my husband was at work, he found a place called NUTS.com. So he would order Skippy five-pound bags of hazelnuts, funny thing, one of my best friends' names was Hazel, too. Anyway, my husband would have them shipped to his work, and he'd bring them home for Skippy. She would go "Nuts" for them. I think we bought her a bag every month, and she'd hide them all over our house.

We would find nuts almost everywhere you could imagine. She put them in our furniture, in our clothing, in our shoes, behind books, in our dressers, in our bed, under the pillows, in our closets, and anywhere and everywhere you could think of, you'd probably find a nut there. My husband and I would be watching TV, and she'd try to stuff a nut in his shirt collar, then she'd run off and get another one, and she'd come running back to hide another one. Funny girl, she was.

When we watched television, she would sit on our feet and watch TV with us. She was part of our family now and turned out to be maybe my best pet I ever had. Once I took her for a ride in my car, and she sat on the dashboard. I only did that once because when I went through the drive-through, she almost jumped out.....never again.

But when my husband would watch football on the weekends, he would share his popcorn with her, or maybe she shared her popcorn with him, I'm not totally sure?? But one thing was for sure, she was always close by and always popping up out of nowhere.

There's A Squirrel In My Kitchen!!

Skippy was a natural at making a nest, too. She discovered toilet tissue one day. We were in the kitchen, and here she came running in the kitchen with a stream of toilet tissue behind her. She would climb the kitchen cabinets and drag the tissue behind her to the top of the cabinets and kind of crush the paper while she was pulling it up at the same time, then she'd climb back down, run to the bathroom, and back up the cabinets in the kitchen until she had her nest complete. Skippy made these in several places in the house.

Over the eight years we had Skippy, as she aged, we continued to let her go out during the days, and when it got dark outside, she always managed to come back home. I knew she loved it outside and was as scared of the cats and hawks out there that I was afraid would get her, so I just couldn't keep her jailed up inside. So I let her run, and out she'd go.

But then "D" day number two came. Skippy went outside as usual. She hung around our backyard most of the time, but this day was different. I had an awful feeling that day. There were a couple of hawks circling around, which worried me to death. Skippy usually came home by dark. Well, it got dark outside, and no sign of Skippy??

I couldn't eat, I was sick to my stomach, worrying if she was ok? My husband said she's probably running around with her friends. Well, six, seven, eight, and nine o'clock went by, still no Skippy? My husband was worrying too, mostly for me, but he sat outside and waited for her to come home. Ten o'clock rolled by! My husband did this thing and made a noise like a clicking sound that Skippy seemed to understand. Well guess what? Shortly after ten, Skippy came down the tree and jumped on my husband's shoulder, and he brought her inside.

Needless to say, that was a long day, my hair is now grayer than blond, and Skippy has seen her last day outside, and I have permanently grounded her forever. Skippy grew older and seemed to be happy just to be inside. She eventually took over my son's clothes dresser. We kept one drawer open, and she made it her newest home.

So, since Skippy became a permanent inside squirrel, she got more interested in the new center of her life, the kitchen. She would watch me as I prepared meals and cooked lunch and dinners for my husband. I would give her some of her vegetables she liked. Some of her favorites were broccoli, carrots, celery, kidney beans, mushrooms, and she loved sweet corn the best.

Her days were full of running and hiding nuts. Building her nests and watching a little television with me before she took her daily nap. I felt so much more at ease when Skippy was inside these days. No worrying if she'd come home or a hawk would carry her away. I still study the

Bible and read countless Christian books, and I always take time to pray. Skippy always kept an eye on me, too. In fact, one day I was praying, and Skippy was nearby. As I was about to finish with my prayers, I looked up, and Skippy had her hands together and had been praying with me, to my surprise. I had to grab my phone to take a photo, so you could see how cute she was. I wondered what she was praying for.

And although this little story is really nowhere near all her adventures, it gives you a little taste of how our lives can be changed in a flash and be so much more fun if we just sit back and let nature come to us as Skippy has. And who knows, maybe you'll get a pet squirrel like ours, and you too can say...

"There's a squirrel in my kitchen."

<u>"Skippy"</u>